fred and the pig

SRA McGraw-Hill

Columbus, Ohio

A Division of The McGraw·Hill Companies

Written by
  Siegfried Englemann
  Elaine C. Bruner

Illustrated by
  Kersti Frigell

www.sra4kids.com

SRA/McGraw-Hill

A Division of The McGraw·Hill Companies

Copyright © 1998 by SRA/McGraw-Hill. All rights reserved.
Except as permitted under the United States Copyright Act, no
part of this publication may be reproduced or distributed in any
form or by any means, or stored in a database or retrieval sys-
tem, without prior written permission from the publisher.

Printed in the United States of America.

Send all inquiries to:
SRA/McGraw-Hill
8787 Orion Place
Columbus, OH 43240-4027

ISBN 0-02-674884-3

18 19 20 21 22 23 QST 07 06 05 04

fred was a very smart fox.
every body cāme to him fōr help.
fred sat in the shāde nēar the sīde of
the river. hē sat and reₐd books.

one dāy fred was sittiñg bȳ the sīde of the river rēadiñg a book. a pig cāme up to him. the pig said, "I want to get to the other sīde of the river."

fred asked, "can you swim?"

the pig said, "I can swim, but that is too far fōr mē."

fred said, "if you can not swim to the other sīde of the river, you can māke a bōat."

the pig said, "the bōats that I māke do not flōat. they sink."

fred said, "I will get you to the other sīde of the river if you pāy mē one dollar."

the pig said, "I will give you a dollar."

sō fred got a long bōard. hē set
the bōard down nēar the sīde of the
river. hē tōld the pig to stand on one
end of the bōard. the other end of
the bōard was ōver the water.

fred said to the pig, "you just
kēēp standiñg there and you will bē
on the other sīde of the river very
soon."

fred ran up the hill and jumped.
hē cāme down on the end of the
bōard that was ōver the water. that
end of the bōard went down.

the end of the bōard with the pig
on it went up. and the pig went into
the āir. hē went ōver the river to the
other sīde.

but hē did not come down on the bank of the river. hē cāme down in the top of a greāt trēē. the pig yelled to fred, "I can not get down from hēre."

fred said, "I will get you down from that trēē if you pāy mē one dollar."

the pig said, "whȳ do I have to pāy you another dollar?"

fred said, "you gāve mē a dollar to get you to the other sīde of the river. you are on the other sīde of the river. if you want to get down from that trēē, you will have to pāy mē another dollar."

the pig said, "I will pāy you another dollar. get mē down from hēre."

fred went to the hōme of a big bēₐver. hē said to the bēₐver, "you arₑ not the best wood cutter in the woods. I met a littlₑ bēₐver who can cut wood better than you."

the big bēₐver said, "I am the best wood cutter in the woods. I can cut better than any other bēₐver."

fred said, "I can fīnd a trēē that is too big fōr you to cut down."

the bēₐver said, "I can cut down any trēē in the woods."

fred said, "come with mē. I will shōw you a trēē you can not cut down."

fred shōwed the big bēaver the trēē with the pig in it. fred said, "there is a trēē you can not cut down."

the bēaver went across the river. hē started cutting down the trēē with his tēēth. hē cut and cut. soon hē had cut sō much wood that the trēē started to fall ōver. the pig yelled, "help. I am falling."

the trēē fell, but it fell back across the river. the pig landed nēar the bōard that was on the bank.

the pig yelled at fred, "I do not want to bē on this sīde of the river. I want to bē on the other sīde of the river."

fred said, "you gāve mē a dollar to get you down from the trēē. I got you down from the trēē."

the pig said, "but I do not want to bē on this sīde of the river. I want to bē on the other sīde of the river."

fred said, "pāy mē another dollar and I will get you across the river."

"nō," the pig said. "I do not want to flȳ in the āir. and I do not want to land in the top of a trēē."

fred said, "I will get you across the river. and you will not flȳ in the āir. but you havₑ to pāy mē one mōrₑ dollar."

the pig said, "I will pāy you another dollar."

fred said, "you can walk across the river on the trēē." the trēē had gonₑ across the river. the pig walkₑd on the trēē and went from one sīdₑ of the river to the other sīdₑ of the river.

the trēē is still across the river.
and fred sits nēₐr the trēē. hē sits
and rēₐds. and if some body wants
to gō to the other sīdₑ of the river,
fred says, "pāy mē one dollar and
you can walk across the river on
mȳ trēē."